Sledge
Academy

B B C
CHILDREN'S BOOKS

Pingu and his friends were having a sledge race.

Everybody wanted to win,
so they were all going very fast.

Nearby, the Sledge Academy tutor was teaching some young penguins how to sledge safely.

Until they were
nearly knocked
over by Pingu and
his racing friends!

But the racers didn't notice. They carried on skidding and sliding and covered poor Pingi in snow…

then they whooshed past Pingu's Father
and made him drop all his shopping.

Father was not happy with the naughty penguins.

The tutor said that Pingu should join the
Sledge Academy. Father agreed.

Meanwhile, the race kept going and the sledges were getting faster and faster.

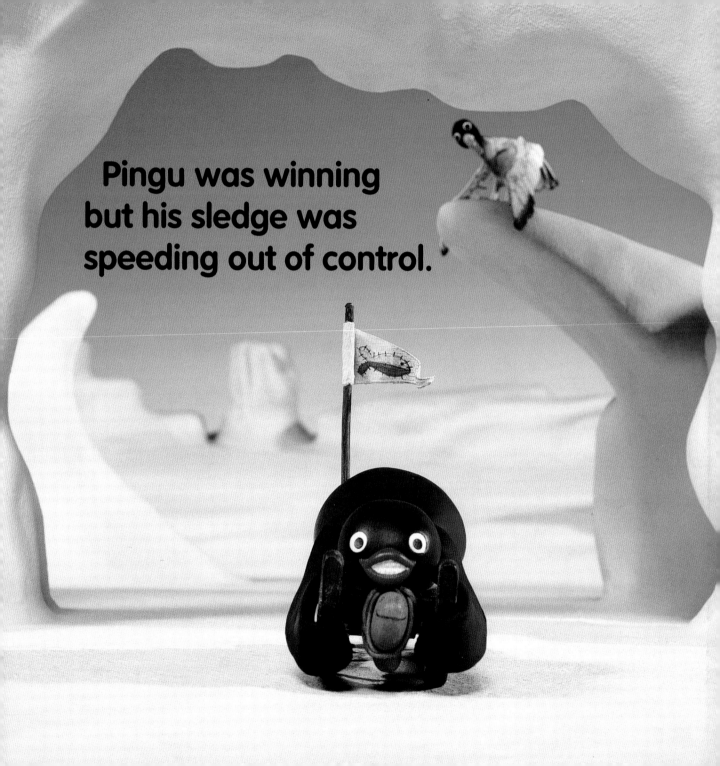

Pingu was winning
but his sledge was
speeding out of control.

The racers were heading towards the fishmonger's stall.

Pongi beeped his horn, but it was too late!

Crash!

The fish went everywhere!

The fishmonger was very cross, so
the naughty penguins rushed away.

Not unless he went to the Sledge Academy to learn how to sledge safely.

Pingu loved sledging, so he agreed to go to the Academy.

At first he found it quite hard…

but with a bit of practice, he soon got the hang of it.

Pingu and his friends were all very proud to pass their sledging tests.

Now they could go sledging whenever they wanted to! Yippee!